W9-AUA-537

PRINCESS Terra AND KING ABADDON

INAUGURAL SERIES: STORY 1
OF THE
GUARDIAN PRINCESSES

This book was produced by the collective work of the Guardian Princess Alliance.

Written by Setsu Shigematsu

Editorial Assistance:
Ilse Ackerman
Ashanti McMillon
Kelsey Moore
Rié Collett
Nausheen Sheikh

Illustrated by A. Das
Preliminary sketches by Leon Chen, Angela Eir,
Yang Liu, Kayla Madison, and Nicole Phung
Voracity illustration (p.32) by Leon Chen

Cover and layout by Vikram Sangha

Common Core questions and activity by Tracy Hualde

Reading level assessment by Candice Herron

ISBN 978-0-9913194-1-1
Library of Congress Control Number: 2013957495

Copyright © 2014
All rights reserved
GPA Press
Printed in the United States of America
First paperback edition

No part of this book may be used or reproduced in any manner without written permission
except in the case of brief quotations in articles and reviews.

PRINCESS Terra AND KING ABADDON

WRITTEN BY
SETSU SHIGEMATSU
& THE GUARDIAN PRINCESS ALLIANCE

ILLUSTRATED BY A. DAS

NCE UPON A TIME in a land called Primos, there lived a princess named Terra. She had wavy golden hair and sparkling green eyes. Princess Terra was the Guardian of the Land. It was her role to protect and care for the land that she loved so dearly. She cherished the flowers, the orchards, and the gardens. She would talk and sing to the beautiful plants and trees. Through her songs, she expressed thanks for the food and wonderful fruits of the land. She thanked the plants for making clean air that kept the people of Primos healthy and happy. Princess Terra would sing:

O Nature so beautiful and bright
Your sun warms us all with its shining light
Meadows of green wonder, fields of golden wheat
Thank you for your wholesome food we eat
Trees of Primos that give us shelter and care
Thank you for the fruit you share

Princess Terra lived among farmers who worked very hard every morning in the fields and orchards. They loved to plant seeds and harvest fruits and vegetables from the bountiful land. Their hard work and fresh food made the people healthy and strong.

In the afternoons, the farmers always made time for some good fun. They would sing:

We love to work hard, and we love to have fun

We dance and play under the big, bright sun

We play with our lutes, wooden flutes, and chimes

With each note in harmony and lyrics that rhyme

We hold festivals to celebrate the changing of the seasons

Our love of the land and music gives us reason

One day, as autumn approached and the leaves turned from green to beautiful shades of yellow, orange, and red, Princess Terra was walking through the woods and came across some strange holes in the ground.

The farmers of Primos would never dig into the Earth with such carelessness. Princess Terra thought to herself, *How unusual. I wonder where these holes came from.* She knelt down to scoop a handful of soil and sang:

> *Sediments, minerals, and deposits of clay*
> *Let the land be healed and loved every day*

She poured the soil from her hand and refilled the holes. Happy that the land was restored, Princess Terra smiled and walked back to the village square.

That same day, while some children of Primos were playing in the woods, they saw a strange man. He was wearing a grey suit that had steel spikes on the shoulders. He had a big crooked grin. As he walked through the land of Primos, he was digging holes everywhere with his strange metal machine.

When Princess Terra heard from the children about this man, she went to the woods to find him.

Upon finding him, Princess Terra kindly said, "Welcome to Primos. What brings you here, and why are you digging holes in our land?"

The man said, "I am Chief Officer Dracos. I have been sent by the mighty King Abaddon, whose power extends across many lands. He is the ruler of Voracity, a land of riches, robots, and machines. We have factories on every corner that work around the clock. We work non-stop to increase our endless stock."

Princess Terra replied, "We've heard of King Abaddon. If your factories run non-stop, when do the people have time to rest and play?"

Dracos ignored her question and instead began speaking about his unusual machine. "My machine can find treasures both new and old. Did you know beneath the ground there is hidden black gold?"

Hearing this, Princess Terra replied, "Yes, we know of the black gold. It has been part of the land from ages past."

Officer Dracos interrupted, saying, "Well, King Abaddon is going to buy your land because he wants more black gold. If you leave, he will offer you this big bag of gold."

Princess Terra politely refused, saying, "No, thank you. We don't need your bag of gold. We do not want to sell our land."

Officer Dracos frowned. He grumbled, "Okay then, the king will offer you two bags of gold."

Princess Terra once again graciously refused. "No, thank you. We want to take care of our land and keep living here for years to come."

Dracos raised his voice. "Fine! I will give you three bags of gold from King Abaddon. This is my final offer!" he said with a huff.

The princess smiled and said, "Officer Dracos, please tell King Abaddon that we do not want his gold." She continued her reply to Dracos with a song:

As we were told from days of old
Our land is never to be sold
Your gold may look shiny and bright
But won't keep us warm for many a night
They won't fill our bodies for very long
But the Earth nurtures us in spirit and song
It gives us all we need to live and love
So this is final; we will not budge

Officer Dracos shouted, "How dare you! Since you've refused my offer, King Abaddon will arrive in seven days with his army of venomous snakes." He sneered, "Let's see if you change your mind when you see the king's snakes slither into your land!" He spat on the ground and stomped away.

Princess Terra thought, *Oh dear, what shall I do? What can we do?* So she went to tell her people about King Abaddon's frightening plan.

That evening, the people gathered around the fire. When the children heard about Officer Dracos and King Abaddon's threat, they asked, "Why is this king so greedy? Why does he want to take our land?"

One of the farmers replied,
"The land of Primos is our home
where our children play and freely roam.
We belong here in this place we hold dear,
on this land that has fed us for hundreds of years."

Although they did not want to leave Primos, the people were very scared of King Abaddon's dangerous snakes. The people of Primos had never seen venomous snakes before, so Princess Terra decided to go to her good friend, Princess Saya, for help. Knowing that there was no time to waste, she quickly got ready. Princess Terra rode her swiftest horse, Majestic Wind, to Princess Saya's land.

Princess Saya lived by a beautiful waterfall at the edge of a rain forest. She was the Guardian of the Lakes and Rivers. She had deep knowledge of reptiles, including those with a venomous bite.

Princess Terra told her friend about King Abaddon's plans. Princess Saya said, "Fear not, my friend. Venomous snakes can be soothed by playing a special song on the flute."

She spent the day teaching Princess Terra how to play a magical song on the flute that had a beautiful soothing melody. Princess Terra practiced and learned it quickly.

She thanked Princess Saya, and they hugged each other good-bye before she rode back to Primos.

As soon as she arrived back in Primos, Princess Terra went to the village. "Everyone, it's time to take out your flutes! I am going to teach you a new song!" she said.

"Princess, how can we enjoy playing music at a time like this? We are so worried that some of us are thinking about fleeing from Primos," a farmer said with a gloomy face. Others were so sad that they had tears in their eyes, for they did not wish to leave their beloved homeland.

Princess Terra said, "Don't worry, my friends. I have learned a special song from Princess Saya that will keep us safe from King Abaddon's snakes." The farmers got their flutes and sat with Princess Terra to learn the new song.

With the day approaching of King Abaddon's frightening arrival, everyone practiced very diligently.

Sure enough, on the seventh day, Officer Dracos and King Abaddon arrived with soldiers carrying large jars of dangerous snakes. The king declared, "Since you did not sell me your land, I am going to release these snakes in Primos and force you to leave. Then, the land will be all mine!"

With trembling hands, the soldiers opened their jars, and hundreds of snakes slithered out. The largest snakes were king cobras, and they were hissing loudly. A few of the soldiers were so scared that they ran away screaming, "AAAHH! HELP!"

The king stood on a platform and declared,

> "These venomous snakes will attack anyone in sight.
> They are under my magic spell to slither and bite.
> I am the mighty King Abaddon, and don't you forget.
> I take everything I want, and whatever I want I get."

To the king's surprise, Princess Terra and the people did not run in fear, but instead they sat bravely as the snakes slithered near. Princess Terra smiled as she took out her flute, and her people followed suit. As they began to play in perfect harmony, the sound grew and grew and grew!

The soothing melody was the most beautiful song they'd ever played. As the sound of music echoed across the hills, the snakes stopped slithering and soon fell asleep. The magical music was able to break the king's evil spell.

The king cried, "What has happened to my dangerous snakes?! They were under my spell. What have you done?!"

He shouted at the remaining soldiers, "Take away their flutes! What are you waiting for?!" The soldiers were hesitant because they too enjoyed the peaceful melody.

As the farmers continued to play the song, Princess Terra said, "King Abaddon, you are not welcome here. It is wrong to use these snakes to carry out your evil deeds. Until you learn to respect all living beings and our way of life, do not return to Primos."

The king said, "You may have outsmarted me, Princess, but this is not the end."
He shouted to Dracos and the soldiers, "Pick up my useless sleeping snakes!"

That very afternoon, King Abaddon returned to Voracity.

The people cheered, "Hooray, the wicked King Abaddon is gone! Hail to Princess Terra and the power of the song!"

Princess Terra humbly said, "Thank you, but I did not do this alone. My good friend, Princess Saya, shared her knowledge and taught me the special song, and you all practiced diligently and performed it beautifully. Let's invite her to our autumn music festival!"

On the day of the festival, as the farmers were preparing for the feast, two of King Abaddon's soldiers nervously crawled out of the nearby bushes. They saw the princess and asked, "Can we stay with you in the land of Primos? We don't want to go back to Voracity. We promise to never harm the people or the land again."

Princess Terra said, "You are welcome to join our community. You must be hungry. Come and eat!"

The soldiers jumped with joy, bowed to the princess, and ran toward the food. During the festival, all the people enjoyed the delicious food that they had prepared for each other. They sang and danced to their hearts' content.

As the festival came to a close, Princess Terra thanked everyone for working together to foil King Abaddon's wicked plan.

She said, "Princess Saya helped us stop the greedy king. Like her, we should also do our best to help and protect others in need." As the sun set over Primos, everyone made a circle, held hands, and sang together in unison:

We pledge to do what is just and fair
To do our best to protect and care
For all living beings great and small have worth
We shall come together to take care of our Earth
We have seen what friendship and unity can bring
We were able to stop the selfish, greedy king
We shall protect the seas, skies, and lands of all nations
To be cherished and shared by the next generations

This became their promise and the new pledge of the Guardian Princesses.

The End

ETYMOLOGY CHART

Etymology: the history of a word

Name	Language	Meaning
Abaddon	Hebrew (Biblical references)	devil, Hell, destruction
Dracos	Latin	dragon
	Greek (related: draconian)	law-giver
Terra	Latin	Earth, land
Primos	Latin	first, at the beginning
Voracity	Latin	extreme appetite, greed

GLOSSARY

Bountiful: large in quantity; plentiful

Cobra: a venomous snake from Asia or Africa that expands the skin of its neck into a hood

Deposits: a collection of minerals in nature (see meaning of minerals)

Diligently: showing great care or determined effort

Foil: to prevent something wrong or undesirable from succeeding

Generations: people born and living during the same time

Graciously: kindly and politely

Lute: a musical instrument that resembles a guitar but has a pear-shaped body

Minerals: a solid substance that is naturally formed by the Earth's processes. It has a particular chemical formula and a crystal structure (for example, turquoise or diamonds)

Rain Forest: a forest with a large amount of rainfall and very tall evergreen trees

Reptiles: cold-blooded animals that lay eggs and have scaly skin (for example, turtles, snakes, alligators, and lizards)

Sediments: stones or sand left by water, wind, or glaciers

Venomous: having or producing venom, which is poisonous fluid made by an animal

COMMON CORE DISCUSSION QUESTIONS

Designed for 3rd grade reading level.

1. Describe Princess Terra. What is her role as a Guardian Princess? Provide evidence in the text to support your answers. (RL.3.3)

2. Look closely at the different illustrations of Primos. List at least three words or phrases from the text that help you describe the setting of this story. (RL.3.1, RL.3.7)

3. The author states, "He had a big crooked grin." What does crooked mean? (RL.3.4) List at least three more words or phrases from the text that describe the character Chief Officer Dracos. (RL.3.1, RL.3.4)

4. Why does the author choose to include King Abaddon's name in the title of her book: *Princess Terra and King Abaddon*? What is his purpose in the story? Use specific details in the story to explain your reason. (RL.3.1, RL.3.3)

5. Reread the song that Princess Terra sings to Officer Dracos regarding the bags of gold on page 14. How does this song explain why Princess Terra refuses the gold? (RL.3.1, RL.3.5)

6. Reread the Guardian Princesses' pledge at the end of the story. What conclusions can you make about what is important to the princesses? Provide evidence from several parts of the story to support your answer. (RL.3.3, RL.3.5)

7. What is the author's central message or lesson in *Princess Terra and King Abaddon*? Be sure to use key details in the story to prove your thinking. (RL.3.2)

COMMON CORE ACTIVITY

Would you rather live in Voracity or Primos?

Be sure to check the Etymology chart to investigate the meaning of their names as well. (RL.3.1) Make sure to write your opinion in the topic sentence, support your opinion with at least two reasons, and make sure to have a concluding statement. (W.3.1a, W.3.1b, W.3.1d)